MW00977053

BRITISH SHORTHAIR CATS

KATIE LAJINESS

Big Buddy Books
An Imprint of Abdo Publishing
abdopublishing.com

BIG BUDDY CATS

abdopublishing.com

Published by Abdo Publishing, a division of ABDO, PO Box 398166, Minneapolis, Minnesota 55439.
Copyright © 2018 by Abdo Consulting Group, Inc. International copyrights reserved in all countries.
No part of this book may be reproduced in any form without written permission from the publisher.
Big Buddy Books™ is a trademark and logo of Abdo Publishing.

Printed in the United States of America, North Mankato, Minnesota.
092017
012018

THIS BOOK CONTAINS
RECYCLED MATERIALS

Cover Photo: Getty Images.
Interior Photos: Getty Images (pp. 5, 7, 9, 11, 13, 15, 17, 19, 21, 23, 27, 29, 30); Tierfotoagentur/R.
    Richter (p. 25).

Coordinating Series Editor: Tamara L. Britton
Contributing Editor: Jill Roesler
Graphic Design: Jenny Christensen

Publisher's Cataloging-in-Publication Data

Names: Lajiness, Katie, author.
Title: British shorthair cats / by Katie Lajiness.
Description: Minneapolis, Minnesota : Abdo Publishing, 2018. | Series: Big buddy cats |
    Includes online resources and index.
Identifiers: LCCN 2017943931 | ISBN 9781532111976 (lib.bdg.) | ISBN 9781614799047 (ebook)
Subjects: LCSH: British shorthair cat--Juvenile literature. | Cats--Juvenile literature.
Classification: DDC 636.82--dc23
LC record available at https://lccn.loc.gov/2017943931

CONTENTS

A POPULAR BREED

Cats are popular pets. About 35 percent of US households have a cat. And, Americans own more than 85 million!

Around the world, there are more than 40 **domestic cat breeds**. One of these is the British shorthair cat. Let's learn why the British shorthair is one of the most popular cat breeds in the United States.

4

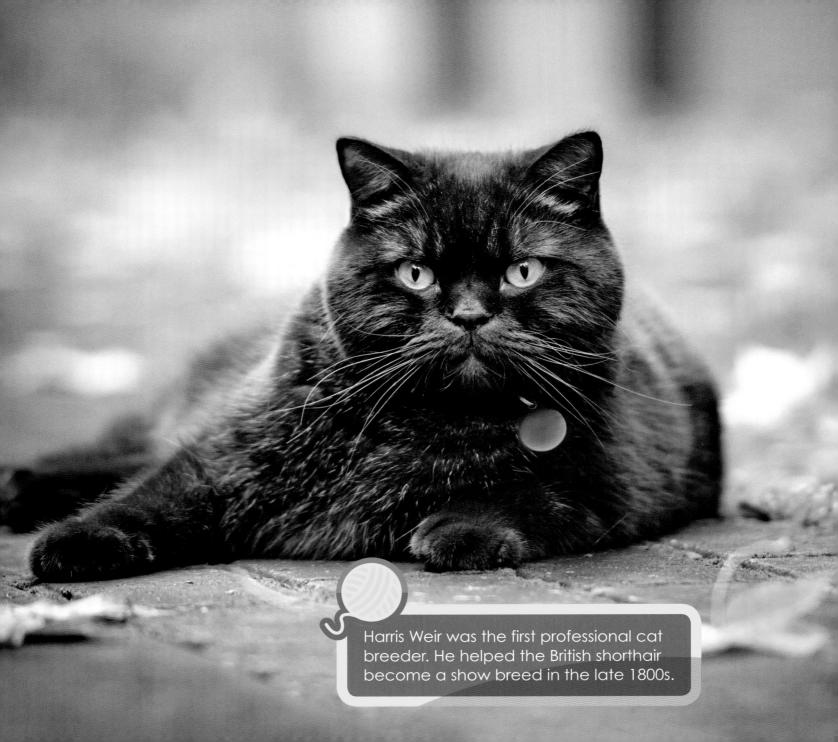

Harris Weir was the first professional cat breeder. He helped the British shorthair become a show breed in the late 1800s.

THE CAT FAMILY

All cats belong to the **Felidae** family. There are 37 **species** in this family. **Domestic cats** are part of one species. Lions and other types of cats make up the others.

Did you know?

Humans and cats have lived together for at least 3,500 years.

Cats purr when they are happy. But, they also purr when they are unhappy. Sometimes cats even purr when they are sick or giving birth.

BRITISH SHORTHAIR CATS

The British shorthair **breed** started in Rome, Italy. Later, the Romans attacked Britain. They brought cats along to protect their food.

After that, British shorthairs wandered the streets of Britain. Over time, people bred these cats to meet certain standards. During the mid-1800s, these well-bred cats began appearing in cat shows.

The British shorthair appeared in early cat shows. It was there that this cat received purebred status.

During **World War II**, food was limited. Many people were unable to feed their cats. So, they owned fewer British shorthairs.

After the war, the **breed** grew popular again. From the 1960s to the 1980s, the British shorthair joined different cat breed **registries**.

The grinning Cheshire cat in *Alice in Wonderland* is a British shorthair cat.

WHAT THEY'RE LIKE

British shorthairs are calm, easygoing cats. They are very loving toward their owners.

Although they have a laid-back nature, British shorthairs are strong, powerful hunters. These **instincts** come from their **ancestors** who caught mice and rats on ships.

British shorthairs do not meow very much. They are rather quiet cats.

COAT AND COLOR

Most British shorthairs are grayish blue. Other common colors include white, black, and cream. They can also have **tabby** and **calico** patterns.

These cats have short, thick coats. This helps keep them warm during cold winters.

A British shorthair's eyes can be copper, blue, green, gold, or hazel. The eye color depends on the coat color or pattern.

SIZE

British shorthairs are medium-sized cats. Adult males weigh 12 to 20 pounds (5 to 9 kg). The females are somewhat smaller at 8 to 14 pounds (4 to 6 kg).

These cats stand 16 to 20 inches (30 to 36 cm) tall at the shoulder. The **breed** has a round head, eyes, and body.

The British shorthair is fully grown by three years old.

FEEDING

Healthy cat food includes beef, chicken, or fish. A good name-brand food will provide the **nutrients** a cat needs.

Cat food can be dry, semimoist, or canned. Food labels will show how much and how often to feed a cat.

Did you know?
Some cats can make more than 100 different sounds!

Cats should not be free fed. Kittens need to eat at least twice a day. Adult cats can eat once a day.

CARE

Cats need regular care to keep them healthy. The British shorthair's smooth coat is simple to **groom**.

A cat should have its claws trimmed every ten to 14 days. A scratching post can help a cat keep its claws short.

Did you know?
Cats can pull back their front claws. This way, they will not scratch anyone while playing.

Most cats do not need baths. Cats spend up to 50 percent of their waking time grooming.

British shorthairs need a good veterinarian. The vet can provide health exams and **vaccines**. He or she can also **spay** or **neuter** cats.

Kittens need to see the vet several times during their first few months. Adult cats should visit the vet once a year for a checkup.

Cats need their ears checked regularly. If the ears look dirty, wipe them with a cotton ball. Then clean them with a product suggested by the vet.

Cats have an **instinct** to bury their waste. So, cats should use a **litter box**. Waste should be removed from the box daily.

A cat buries its waste to mark its area. If a cat goes outdoors, it will begin to do the same. A **microchip** can help bring a cat home if it gets lost.

Each domestic cat should have its own litter box, plus one extra. For homes with many levels, keep a litter box on each floor.

KITTENS

A British shorthair mother is **pregnant** for 63 to 65 days. Then, she gives birth to a **litter** of about five kittens. For the first two weeks, kittens mostly eat and sleep.

All kittens are born blind and deaf. After two weeks, they can see and hear. At three weeks, the kittens begin taking their first steps.

Cats are still kittens until they are one year old.

THINGS THEY NEED

Between 12 and 16 weeks old, British shorthair kittens are ready for **adoption**. Kittens like to be active. So, they need daily exercise. A British shorthair cat will be a loving companion for about 20 years.

Older cats and kittens may not get along. Older cats do not like change.

GLOSSARY

adoption the process of taking responsibility for a pet.

ancestor a family member from an earlier time.

breed a group of animals sharing the same appearance and features. To breed is to produce animals by mating.

calico a blotched or spotted animal.

domestic cats tame cats that make great pets.

Felidae the scientific Latin name for the cat family. Members of this family are called felines. They include domestic cats, lions, tigers, lynx, and cheetahs.

groom to clean and care for.

instinct a way of behaving, thinking, or feeling that is not learned, but natural.

litter all of the kittens born at one time to a mother cat.

litter box a place for house cats to leave their waste.

microchip an electronic circuit placed under an animal's skin. A microchip contains identifying information that can be read by a scanner.

neuter (NOO-tuhr) to remove a male animal's reproductive glands.

nutrient (NOO-tree-uhnt) something found in food that living beings take in to live and grow.

pregnant having one or more babies growing within the body.

registry a place where official records are kept.

spay to remove a female animal's reproductive organs.

species (SPEE-sheez) living things that are very much alike.

tabby a domestic cat with a striped and spotted coat.

vaccine (vak-SEEN) a shot given to prevent illness or disease.

World War II a war fought in Europe, Asia, and Africa from 1939 to 1945.

ONLINE RESOURCES

Booklinks
NONFICTION NETWORK
FREE! ONLINE NONFICTION RESOURCES

To learn more about British shorthairs, visit **abdobooklinks.com**. These links are routinely monitored and updated to provide the most current information available.

INDEX